Squeak's Good Idea

For Tom and Danny
∾ M. E.

For Alexander Agnew
P. B. ∾

Text copyright © 2001 by Max Eilenberg
Illustrations copyright © 2001 by Patrick Benson

First U.S. edition 2001

Library of Congress Cataloging-in-Publication Data

Eilenberg, Max.
Squeak's good idea / written by Max Eilenberg ; illustrated by Patrick Benson. — 1st U.S. ed.
p.   cm.
Summary: When Squeak the elephant decides to go outside for a picnic
he prepares himself for any eventuality, which turns out to be a good idea.
ISBN 0-7636-1591-9
[1. Preparedness — Fiction. 2. Elephants — Fiction.] I. Benson, Patrick, ill. II. Title.
PZ7.E3443 Sq 2001
[E] — dc21   00-066726

10 9 8 7 6 5 4 3 2 1

Printed in Italy

This book was typeset in Minion Condensed.
The illustrations were done in pen, ink, and watercolor.

Candlewick Press
2067 Massachusetts Avenue
Cambridge, Masssachusetts 02140

visit us at www.candlewick.com

Squeak's
Good Idea

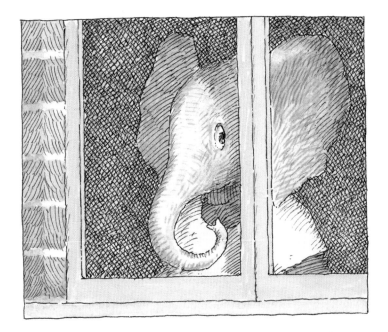

Max Eilenberg
pictures by Patrick Benson

CANDLEWICK PRESS
CAMBRIDGE, MASSACHUSETTS

"I've got a good idea," said Squeak.

"Let's all go out. Who wants to come?"

"I'm busy," said Poppa.

Momma and Tumble were busy too.

"Oh," said Squeak.

"Then I'll have

to go by myself."

He opened the door
and looked out.
"Hmm," he said.
"It might be cold."

So he went to the closet
and got his jacket.
And then, just to be on the safe
side, he got his mittens, his hat,
and his warmest pants as well.
"Momma," he called.
"May I borrow your scarf?"

"Of course you may,"
said Momma.

Squeak went back to the door.

He looked out.

"Hmm," he said.

"It might rain."

So he went to the hall and got his raincoat. And then, just to be on the safe side, he got his boots and some extra socks as well.

"Poppa," he called. "May I borrow your umbrella?"

"Of course you may," said Poppa.

Squeak went back to the door.

He looked out.

"Hmm," he said.

"I might get hungry."

So he went to the kitchen
and got some cookies.
And then, just to be on the safe side,
he got some bread and some apples
and a basket to carry them in.
"What are you doing?" asked Tumble.

"I thought," said Squeak,
"I might have a picnic."

Squeak went back to the door.

He looked out.

"Hmm," he said.

"I'm ready."

Squeak stepped outside.

"That's a pretty flower," he said.

"What a noisy bee."

Squeak walked, one step at a time,

to the tree at the end of the garden.

"Hmm," said Squeak.
  He put down his basket.
  "It's not at all cold—and
  it's certainly not rainy."

So he pulled off his boots,
and his mittens and his hat,
and his extra socks,
and his raincoat and his jacket,
and his warmest pants,
and he tied Momma's scarf
to Poppa's umbrella
and he hung them
from the tree.

"Good," said Squeak.

He looked at his basket.

"Now it's time for my ..."

"**PICNIC!**" yelled Tumble.

"I'm glad you've come," said Squeak.

"This was a good idea," said Momma.

"I love picnics!" said Tumble.

"Lucky you brought so many things," said Poppa.

"Yes," said Squeak. "It's best to be on the safe side."

And everyone agreed that it was.